THE CRUMPLED KREEPITS
Kitty Karen and Ken

Fred and Francis FRIZZEL

Bette BILLYBUNK

Ernie QUILCH

Ron PLUMPKIN

Tony and Tilly TRIBBLE

Wilma YUMPTEE

© 1996 Graham Percy

Book design by The Artworks Press
Jacket design by Jennifer West

Typeset in Monotype Gill Sans Light
The illustrations in this book were created using crayon and ink.
Printed in Hong Kong

Library of Congress Cataloging-in-Publication Data
Percy, Graham.
24 Strange little animals in a haunted house / Graham Percy.
p.   cm.
Summary: When the bus they are riding on breaks down, a group of unusual
creatures must spend the night in a deserted house where everything seems
very frightening—until the following morning.
ISBN: 0-8118-1035-6
[1. Haunted houses—Fiction. 2. Monsters—Fiction.]
I. Title.
PZ7.P4246A14   1996
[E]—dc20   96-5208
CIP   AC

Distributed in Canada by Raincoast Books
8680 Cambie Street
Vancouver B.C. V6P 6M9

Distributed in Australia and New Zealand
by CIS Cardigan Street
245-249 Cardigan Street, Carlton 3053 Australia

10 9 8 7 6 5 4 3 2 1

Chronicle Books
275 Fifth Street
San Francisco, CA 94103

For Rachel and Alexander – G. P.

Graham Percy

24 strange little animals

THE HAUNTED HOUSE

chronicle books

San Francisco

One weekend, twenty-four strange little animals rented an old bus for a journey to the hills.

"I've found a cozy little hotel where we can stay," said Ernie Quilch who was driving the bus. "I think we're nearly there."

Mrs. Tribble was sitting up front. She looked out from behind an enormous road map and whispered, "Ernie . . . there's a hill up there, but it isn't on the map . . . I think we're lost!"

Just then there was an awful gg*runch*ing noise and a puff of steam as the bus *Skreek*ed to a stop. Suddenly everything was quiet. In the woods an owl h0000ted.

The Sugareenoes rubbed circles on the misty glass of their window.

"It's very dark out there," said Sammy.

"It's very wet out there," said Sylvester.

Suzy Sugareeno pulled open a side window and put her nose out just a little. "And it's very cold," she squeaked, pulling her nose in quickly.

Izzy Inkstump turned up his collar, got off the bus, and stood on the muddy road. He looked up the hill. Then he climbed back onto the bus and announced, "There is a house up on the hill. Wilma Yumptee and Ernie Quilch will stay down here with me and we'll try to fix the bus.

The rest of you put on warm clothes, take some blankets, and go up to the house. I'm sure they will let you wait there while we work on the engine."

Charlie Chump led them all in line up the hill. They slid and slipped and stumbled and scrambled and finally reached the house. Everyone clustered around a tree stump.

"There aren't any lights on," whispered Quincy to Queenie Quincepig. Charlie wrapped his arms around them and, looking over to Ron Plumpkin, said, "Go up and see if there's anyone at home."

When Ron knocked on the front door, it creaked open. He looked in nervously. Then he turned and called softly down to the huddle of little animals.

"There's no one here. Come on up!"

The twenty-one strange little animals tiptoed up the steps but no one wanted to be the first to go inside the gloomy house. "It's all right," said Charlie. "I'm sure the owners wouldn't mind us taking shelter in here on such a wet and windy night."

The Crumpled Kreepits had a small flashlight. Karen held it above her head, and all the animals went into the front hall of the house. The house was full of furniture. There were curtains, books, and pictures on the walls. Then Karen Kreepit's flashlight went out. "Oh no!" she gasped. "The batteries are dead!"

"I think we should all spread out and find somewhere to sleep," said Cal Cushiontop with a yawn. Then he plumped down in a heap under the stairs. Mrs. Grizzle and the little Grizzles lay down beside him.

The others went off to find a place to sleep. Some went downstairs and some upstairs and soon whispering could be heard throughout the dark house. Finally everyone found a place to lie down and the whispering stopped. All was quiet . . . and then a pale, ghostly light began to shine.

"YEEEEK!" screamed the Grizzles. "There's a snake! There's a snake and it's going for Mr. Cushiontop!"

"OHHHHH!" came a wail from the living room. "There's a rhinoceros and it's about to charge."

"AAAAAARGH!" choked the Kreepits, as an awful clawed creature arched its back to spring at them.

Upstairs the Tribbles yowled, "There's a giant at the end of the bed!"

"And . . . it's . . . got . . . t . . . t . . . two heads!" gasped Ron Plumpkin.

"YUUUUUUGH," groaned the Quincepigs and the Frizzels. "There's a HUGE spider with hundreds of legs climbing up the walls."

Downstairs, Charlie Chump was wondering what all the commotion was about. Suddenly, he wailed, "WHEEEEEEE! This house is haunted!"

All at once the moon disappeared behind the clouds and it was dark in the house again. The twenty-one strange little animals rushed to the front door and landed in a quivering heap on the veranda outside.

"Let's all just stay together," gasped Charlie, slamming the front door firmly behind him.

They tumbled down the hill where they found a leafy hollow to hide in. There, they all curled up to sleep, except for Charlie and Cal, who stayed awake keeping an eye on the house.

It was just getting light when Izzy, Wilma and Ernie climbed up the hill from the road singing cheerily, "We've fixed the bus . . . we've fixed the bus . . ."

When they stumbled upon their friends sleeping in the hollow, their singing suddenly stopped.

"What on earth are you all doing here?" asked Izzy.

They all started talking at once.

"It's haunted . . . the house is haunted!" they cried.

"Nonsense," said Izzy, as he set off towards the house. The others trailed nervously behind him.

As Izzy reached the steps, Cal Cushiontop pushed past him and threw himself, arms outstretched, across the front door. He begged Izzy not to go into the house.

"There's a very hungry snake under the stairs," he pleaded.

"And a huge, crazy rhinoceros in the living room," the Sugareenoes joined in.

"And a beast with long, sharp claws," added the Kreepits.

"And a two-headed giant," groaned Ron Plumpkin.

"And a huge spider with hundreds of legs," howled the Quincepigs.

"And what's more," added Charlie Chump, "a grinning ghoul."

"I saw it with my very own eyes!" added Cal.

"Well, I'm going to see all this with my very own eyes!" said Izzy. Then he pushed the front door open.

Izzy went straight to where Cal and the Grizzles had been under the stairs.

"I suppose this is your poisonous snake," he said, smiling.

Then Izzy strode into the living room and stopped in front of some furniture draped with sheets. He bent down and whispered to the little Sugareenoes, "Could this be the charging rhinoceros?"

Izzy sat down on a chair at the end of the room. He looked at all the things on the desk in front of him, and spun around to face the Crumpled Kreepits. "Could this be your awful clawed creature?" he asked.

Then they all went upstairs. Only Izzy dared to go into the first bedroom.

"I guess that must be the two-headed giant."

The Quincepigs dragged him to the doorway of the second bedroom.

"You're very clever, Izzy Inkstump, but the monster in there isn't still . . . it moves."

Izzy bravely opened the door . . . just a little . . . and peeped into the room. Just then, the wind blew the branches of an old oak tree and their shadows danced around the walls. He turned and smiled.

"Is this the spider with hundreds of legs?"

By now everyone was looking very embarrassed. Only Charlie Chump and the Slumpstumps still looked worried.

"You still haven't explained away the grinning ghoul we saw," they said pointing down the stairs.

Izzy squeezed past them and bounded down the stairs. There was a pause. Then they could hear him laughing.

They all pushed forward and looked down to where Izzy was standing. He pointed at a cage with two little birds happily perching inside.

Sandy and Sophie Slumpstump laughed and looked over at Charlie who was grinning sheepishly.

Now everyone was happy. They all marched out of the house and down the hill. Ernie Quilch started to sing, making up the words as he went along:

"There's no such thing as a purple mouse . . ."
and everyone joined in:
"There's no such thing as a haunted house."

When they reached the road, Izzy revved up the old bus and the twenty-four strange little animals drove off into the sunrise.

Sandy and Sophie SLUMPSTUMP

The GRIZZLES
Gracey
Garth and Gwen

Sammy Sylvester and Suzy SUGAREENO

Izzy INKSTUMP

Charlie CHUMP

Cal CUSHIONTOP

Quincy QUINCEPIG

Queenie QUINCEPIG